GOD STRIKE

1

JOSE NIEVES

Godstrike

Episode 1: Life Changing fate

Warning:Cursing
PS:this has nothing to do with any other
product, Just the title
Author: Jose Nieves

Warriors are born in mysterious ways, some triumph and others fall, but the greatest become legends. My name is Jose and this is my strange story on how I became one. My story starts off pathetic as I ended up dying trying to save my sister. There was an earthquake during our vacation and the house fell on top of me, but it was quick and painless so I guess that's a plus maybe. I don't know what exactly happened when i died but when I woke up I was in heaven. Suddenly I saw a figure emerge from the cloud in front of me "who's there, show yourself right now" I demanded "Do not threat Jose, for I am who I am" and as the figure got closer and closer I felt a massive amount of pressure, but in a comforting sort of way and the figure emerged as it was the one and only god. That's right the Father of Jesus standing right before me and I tried to attack him, god I'm stupid.

"Who are you?" I asked, "Don't threaten Jose, I am god, creator of everything" he said, and "Of course I bowed down because he's superior to anything". Wow i honestly can't believe that I'm seeing you, i mean i pray to you but i never thought you were actually real" i said "of course I'm real and I've been watching you, and honestly i have mixed feelings about you especially how you act" God said "honestly i can't blame you i just have issues with kids who are absolute distractions and i also have trust issues ever since 2014 when my cousin wouldn't let me play a video game i seriously wanted to play." I said "i can't blame you Jose i see how those kids seriously are and how they pick on your friends and not give a crap about me" God replied "wow god just wow, so can you probably resurrect me please" "1st of all that's not a bad word and sure since you died as a kid" so god resurrected me and i dug out of the damn grave {god it was hard} and when my family saw me alive they hugged me so hard and cried which felt weird but understandable. What pissed me off was that they sold my phone, but eventually they bought me a new and better phone which was a galaxy s20++

When I went to school everyone was shocked to see me, for the entire bus ride I was barraged by a swarm of questions, but I just remained silent because I don't give a damn. It never stopped even the teachers were also asking me questions along with even more students as I punched kicked and clawed my way out of questions as I hate paparazzi. The positive thing is people kept giving me a whole load of snacks considering I must have gotten some sort of depression so I got snacks of all kinds. The day after I came to school I had gym class my bully who we shall refer to as Tyler S wanted to pick a fight like all bullies do as he says "So considering you survived the debts of hell, you should survive this brutal beating" I enjoy fighting but I'm still not in the mood. He pushed me which ticked me off so I punched him through the roof. Everyone stared in silence as I looked in my hands and whispered "I have powers." I began panicking and running around, but then I knocked myself out with the wall.

I woke up at the nurse's office moaning "uhhh what happened?" I asked "you knocked yourself out by running into the wall, thankfully nothing's broken or injured" the nurse confirmed "You should leave because the bus arrived 5 minutes ago" "S--- Thanks "I exclaimed and ran outside towards the busses. When I got home I went to my backyard and Said "God do you know how the heck I was able to uppercut someone through a roof, and soon after I was beamed to god's palace in front of god's throne. "Jose I think it's time I mentioned something important" I Listened and this is what he told me "A long time ago heaven has been at war with Hell and its demons, the battle was gruesome and many angels died and many died, but some soldiers had special powers to combat these warriors, 1 of these soldiers had the ability of light and which was inherited to you, it just never became active until now" "Holy Jesus, that is insane" I exclaimed "yes Jose but be careful for a new threat is coming and God sent me back.

After hearing all that I was shocked, confused and excited so I decided to call up a friend to begin training to use my powers. 1st test was to test out projectiles so I had to throw balls of light energy against a tower of cups and each of them disintegrated. 2nd was hand to hand combat, normally I would spar with Joey but because I was on a whole different tier I just had multiple punching bags, I blindfolded myself and took on all of them at the same time and punched some of them so hard it left the stratosphere. Next up is speed and flight, so after running normally for 10 minutes which exhausted the hell out of me I began running a lot faster than the naked eye and I flew upwards like 20 feet only for me to fall flat on my butt. Finally was strength as Joey took me to the tallest mountain in Maryland "is that the tallest?" I asked "hey man be grateful since I'm helping you" Joey demanded so I destroyed it into pebbles with a 1 inch punch. Afterwards I decided to turn pieces of paper into $100 dollar bills and we went to buy even more snacks.

A few days later it was lunch time and Joey told me he uploaded the test on YouTube and now he's YouTube famous. That was short lived as an alarm went off and Dr. Lionce said that there was a school shooter in the building. Everyone like wimps ran screaming i knew this was my chance but Dr. Lionce tried to stop me saying "Jose what are you doing? Are you trying to get killed? You're just a kid!" "Trust me i aint no ordinary kid" i replied with red fire in my hand. A minute later i found the shooter "god damn it" i said as the shooter had Jordan and literally tried to shoot me "JOSE!" Jordan yelled but the bullet landed on the ground and I was absolutely fine and Joey saw the whole thing. Apparently I'm bulletproof and Joey recorded the guy constantly shooting me with no success, so i saved my best friend, beat the guy to pulp, and brought him the police tied up and the whole school saw me with the criminal in my hands. The police arrested the man and all the school literally carried me up and chanted "Jose" over and over again. Yeah I'm awesome

When my parents found out they were in shock and proud of me. They took me to get KFC and Popeye which was awesome since i love those places and i ate a bunch of chicken. 4 buckets which was the $20 dollar pick up alongside the mashed potatoes. As for Popeye i ate 4 orders of the family meal which was 56 pieces of chicken and 7 biscuits along with coleslaw, a ton of Cajun fries and mashed potatoes. {I eat what I want damn it unless I'm forced to eat it} Around 9am since it's a Friday i went outside looked up in the sky and thanked God for these powers, but he reassured me that i shouldn't thank him yet because a greater evil will rise. He was right as Satan was looking at what was happening and said "So my nemesis has a new champion, heh, no matter he won't stop me from taking over this world" "Get the armies ready!" He yelled at a henchmen "it's time for Satan to Rise! Mwahahahaha!" Satan laughed.

The End!

God Strike
Earth's Defender

Episode 2:Rise of an enemy

By Jose Nieves

PS don't worry it's free
PSS:i forgot to mention there's some mild if
not strong language

A week passed, and I decided to tell my secret to someone you least expect, Tyler Rizenhour "what? Jose that's so ridiculous," Tyler said when I told him. "Oh yeah, well if i didn't have powers how am i able to do this!" i said taking a bottle cap and flicking at fast speed which hit almost everyone in guitar class, so fast Ms. Louder didn't notice. "Ya see!" i said "wow" Tyler replied "that's not all!" i said pausing time then hitting Austin's head like a drum then slapping him before i said "sorry". "Okay, i believe you" Tyler said "wanna go get slurpees?" I asked "sure" Tyler replied and we got some. "Hey god" i asked late in the day "what exactly is the purpose for these powers" "Jose" god says "everything i do has a purpose, just wait for tomorrow you'll get your answer" and god vanished. After that conversation, I stayed up as I didn't know what he meant but tomorrow I found what he meant.

Ps sorry Tyler if i got your last name wrong

One day while I was in town, I heard a siren and it was coming from the bank so I rushed toward there and hid in an alley. What I saw was a group of men and their leader putting money in a van and driving at full throttle. After a minute the police were in pursuit and I was following through the rooms of buildings and eventually the police lost them. "Oh screw it" I said and jumped and ran towards the criminals who stopped. When I landed I took down the men 1 by 1 then there was only one left. When I was punching and kicking him, he barely flinched then he punched me and it actually did damage. Then he threw me into a wall then blasted me with a laser that basically overpowered me. The guy then walked towards and looked at me then said "you got guts kid, I guess that's why god chose you" I was confused so I asked "who the hell are you" he replied with "me, oh just called me Darkron, Satan told me about you and he was pretty right, but kid just go home" and Darkron left and I was just sitting in a wall when eventually God beamed me up to heaven for something important, and no I didn't die I was just beamed up cause i didn't have energy by myself.

Thanks god" I said after he healed me "but I still got my a--whooped" "I know I saw the whole thing" god replied with "Jose, the world you know isn't what you think it is, Satan has plans, he's making preparations" he said. "So what do you propose I should do?" I said "that is for you to decide" God said and sent me back. Since then I've been thinking which lead to a flashback: the flashback was when i was in Puerto Rico when I was a kid I was getting bullied by this one kid until i decided to start fighting back, i was in the wall he was kicking me so I grabbed his foot slammed his face into the ground and started punching without mercy then karate chopped his neck then high kneed his jaw, breaking it then kicked him to finally get him down, which hospitalized him but he never bullied me again. After remembering this I decided what to do, so one day in school I went up to Tyler and said "I need you for something" and he made me a super suit and we showed it to god "impressive, what's gonna be your name?" God asked "how about. ...... Godstrike" I said

The mission of getting back at the criminal gang started at night, while I was on a rooftop Tyler was talking to me and threw an earpiece. "Alright Jose, I've spotted the criminals so head to these coordinates" I agreed and looked at all the buildings and sprinted across the roof and descended down {i was in the moment} but when I got a grip I grew angel wings and flew up then did a another backflip and started running on cars. Then flew up and started wall jumping on buildings then running on the rooftops until I finally stopped on the tallest building in Baltimore as it was exhausting parkour and only seconds when I was done Tyler decided to not let me rest and said "are you done?" and replied with "yeah yeah I'm fine just tired, let's do this" so after 5 minutes of breathing i got a grip and headed straight towards the base of the criminal gang. While making sure no one saw me, because I'm pretty sure vigilantes are illegal.

"Alright you idiots, nice job with the robbery today" Darkron said. After the criminals had a beer or 2, all the lights turned off and I landed on the ground. Now Tyler made my suit golden which sucks for stealth so the men saw me so I had to fight. Multiple men went at me at once but I took them down in a few blows and broke some of their body parts until the only 1 left was Darkron. "Well Darkron, you were right for Satan, to think I'm a challenge" i said "please i 'll take you down in a matter of seconds" he said "bring it" i replied and the fight began. It began with us exchanging blows then we both punched that blew us back then fired projectiles at each other. Then charged at each other, he punched me but i powered through it and kicked him in the stomach then landed an uppercut which broke through the roof and a couple of windows since we were in a warehouse, i followed him up there and he got up easily so the fight continued.

We rushed at each other with blow after blow but Darkron dodged and then started barraging me with blows and multiple energy blast, but I teleported and delivered blows while teleporting then hit him with another uppercut and filled my hand full of aura and whispered "Sayonara sucker" and with that I jumped up and punched him in the gut then a Giant laser fired sending him out of the stratosphere which then not only burns him alive BUT CUTS THE FREAKING SUN IN HALF!. The battle was over, but it was so intense I screamed and roared wildly "RAAAAAAHHHHHHHHHHH!" That was interrupted when I heard a siren "crap the cops" So I teleported out of there. When the cop entered the warehouse all they found was the men knocked out and tied up with a note on the wall saying 'your welcome - Godstrike', I ended up on a rooftop and looked at the entire city in the distance while whispering the words "It Begins"

The next day while I was in school and was heading into guitar class, Tyler pulled me aside. "Dude what's up?" I asked "HAVE YOU SEEN THE NEWS!" he said loudly, so we went to the computer lab and Mr. Palo let us watch it in 1 of his computers and this is what we saw "Breaking news the criminal gang known as the snakes have been arrested and it appears we have a vigilante in town, let's go to the scene of the crime. There is it, the message on the wall now let's go to an interview with someone who saw the thing" and it went to a random person "I saw 2 figures on a roof then a yellow light on the same area that lasted for 2-3 minutes" "well there you go a vigilante is in town everyone, more on the story as it develops". "Well now everyone knows about you!" Tyler said "well no one knows who i am so were still clear" i said. Meanwhile in hell Satan watched the whole thing "impressive, since none of my minions can do anything, might as well give this kid a little challenge" Satan said with wine in his hands.

GodStrike
Earth's Defender

Episode 3:The Dog Of Lightning Kazuma

By Jose Nieves

PS don't worry it's free
PSS:i forgot to mention there's some mild if
not strong language

After the news report the whole topic of Godstrike has been blowing up everywhere even in school they've been talking about me, but I can't say anything at all. So after school god asked me to visit him for something important, so after teleporting to heaven Tyler and I met up with God. We bowed and asked "you wanna see us God" "yes, now that you got your grips together we have work to do" he replied "what kind of work?" I asked "a long time ago when I created the continents I hid special weapons: The claws of lightning, The blades of fire, The trident of water, The kunai of poison, The axe of ice and the hammer of earth. When all these weapons are combined they hold the key to untold power". "So you want me to go find these weapons all across the world" I asked "yes but we must hurry Satan's men will stop at nothing to prevent you from finding it" God said "alright then let's do this" I said full of excitement while God looked at Tyler and Tyler said "yeah he's an idiot".".

"Alright Jose the 1st weapon we're after are the Lightning Claws, located in Lake Maracaibo in Venezuela, South America. The most thundery place in the world and within said place is .... " Tyler explained but I interrupted by saying "The Lightning Temple" but suddenly lightning struck and I jumped up in shock. "Man this place is electric, literally" I joked but then I heard a "RRRRRRRRROOOOOOOOOOOAAAAAAAARRRRRRRRRR R!" "WTF was that!?" I asked then God answered "Sorry I forgot to mention that the weapons themselves are guarded by monsters Satan created so you're going to have to defeat each and every one. Starting with the Lightning dog: Kazuma" and exactly when he said it another thunderbolt struck. "So I take it, it's gonna be video game style?" I asked "Yeah exactly" God said while being unaware "well I don't care because this is only going to deliver the absolute hype" I said as I rushed towards the building.

So when I entered the building the 1st room Satan's men were waiting for me with scythes, so I pulled up my sword and filled my hands with an aura ready to battle. My battle strategy was to slash one enemy at a time and when one enemy tried to attack me I would just backflip and keep them away with my fireballs, but after trying that I decided to pull off aerial combos with my sword along with shooting fireballs in the air as well as I had to do it multiple times as since they come from hell they resurrect. After dealing with these poor suckers the door opened up like a hack n slash game. "okay, time get moving" so being in a temple I had to go through stairs and other ancient rooms , but eventually I made it to a place where basically call platforming. To clarify there's floating rocks that get struck by lightning both on top and below, in these situations you have to memorize the pattern especially there's a ton of sections of floating rocks where each one has more rocks. You get used to it, but eventually I have to use my wings to cross more distance..

So after entering the garden room I met a new kind of enemy called the Light-rage as they seem pissed and they don't really have weapons they only fight with their fist. They also have charging fist attacks so I had to dodge that, but instead of resurrection they spawn even more and their sturdy so i did some sick combos, but after some combos I just kept shooting projectiles and eventually I kept going as this place is fully guarded. After going through more rooms I made it to a place where the doors are locked and I have to find an amulet to unlock it. Apparently there's 6 rooms and after going through 5 rooms full of enemies I found the amulet in the 6th nut after getting out of the room I was attacked "BALL LIGHTNING!" I yelled and dodged all of them, but then each of them turned into birds and I called them electro birds. They kept shooting lightning until they came swooping down then I attacked them. After all of them were defeated I put the amulet in the shrine which was in the same room which opened the door.

Okay here's a shock, when the doors opened there were rods of lightning floating "so how do you suppose to get through?" Tyler asked then I looked at my sword then I got an idea. I jumped high and began to ride my sword and grinding on the lightning rods like riding a skateboard. Some of the lightning ended so I had to jump onto another like a pro skater saying stuff like "getting airborne" and "riding crazy" it was pretty awesome until finally I got onto the final lightning rod which made me go faster by the second then going up as the rod was a straight line and jumped high then landed and after getting it together I noticed the lightning dog Kazuma. As I got closer eventually he noticed me and said "Leave at once, no man can have these claws, YOU WILL DIE" I just responded with "oh-ho, easy fella, hey where I come from I see a bunch of doggies who look just like you" "YOU dare mock me, I'll make you perish!" it yelled "you don't go out often huh, come on buddy i 'll take you for a walk, come on, don't be shy" I said "I will EAT YOUR FLESH AND CRUNCH YOUR BONES !" then it broke free and roared and i just said "so you wanna play huh. looks like we're gonna need a bigger leash, bring it".

To start off the match he covered the room in lightning then started shooting it out of his mouth. The fact is about this guy is when he attacks you have to attack him while airborne because the ground leaves you vulnerable as along with shooting lightning kazuma also slashes you with his claws along with charging at you to bite you. Like I said dodge and attack as when he does he's wide open to attack. As if he wasn't hard enough when he's half way of getting defeated he jumps and shoots tons of lightning and strikes at you with his entire body covered in lightning but after that he continues to attack me the same way, but he does that again when at 25% health but eventually I beat him. When he was defeated he exploded then left the claws of lightning, when I touched them they teleported into my hands and guess what. With the claws on I started slashing ahead like a professional then used the lightning abilities within it then I caused a giant thunderbolt behind me and after that I said "I can get used to this" then I teleported out of there.

school next day me and Tyler were eating lunch in an abandoned part of the school to avoid bullies while testing the Lightning claws by shooting lightning at soda cans which exploded and cutting logs of fallen down trees in less than 10 seconds "You never fail to disappoint Jose" Tyler complimented "yeah it's no big deal" I replied "Who would've thought that us, a weeb and a nerd is busy saving the world" I continued "I still can't believe it either but were still far from the end of the tunnel, since there are so many other weapons to gain and Satan's going to be hot on us" Tyler admitted "Yeah but it's not like he's going to stalk us in school after all this is the safe spot" I said "yeah" Tyler breathed. Meanwhile Satan pondered the situation as he began talking "looks like I'm going to have to observe Godstrike from the inside" he then transforms and then transforms into a human while gleaming with joy "Perfect!"

To be continued

GodStrike
Earth's Defender

Episode 4:Burning identity

By Jose Nieves

PS don't worry it's free
PSS:i forgot to mention there's some mild if
not strong language

Normally today would be an ordinary school day, but today it wasn't. Principal Don said through the speakers "students and teachers were having a last minute assembly to introduce our new staff member" usually this would be a good thing but for me it wasn't for me, not at all. When all of 8th grade made it to the cafeteria principal Don started talking "here is our new employee his name is Lucifer and I want everyone to give him a warm welcome" but as soon I heard the name 'Lucifer' I immediately knew it was Satan. After principal Don was finished talking, 'Lucifer' began talking "I must say it's an absolute pleasure to be a school full of geniuses" which already made a bunch of people already like him especially the girls as they all think he's charming "oh brother!" I said furiously and was annoyed going back to class as this son of a b---- can go ahead and fool everyone but not me.

It didn't take long for Lucifer to become popular, to start off he gave everyone ice cream parties every Friday, he gave everyone more cub cash then normal, and let everyone do whatever they want and didn't send anyone out, this guy has no responsibility. To make things worse when I was at lunch I bumped into this guy "oh hey, you must be Jose I heard good things about you" Lucifer said "really, well I'm guessing there right", then we shook hands and then he started whispering "I know your Godstrike Jose, I can't do anything here but one day i 'll get you." I just looked at him angrily and said "trust me I agree with you there as i 'll so kick your a-- just not now" and then we continue to angrily shake hands until finally Lucifer had to leave and when I tried to tell my table it was Satan no one would listen to me, yet I'm the mature one. Eventually Tyler and I did research on him and this is what we found: "Okay Lucifer, born in Los Angeles, owns a bar, part time detective, and slept with... 300 women!" Tyler said "WTF" I said loudly, then Tyler got a message from god as it's time to get the next weapon: The Blades of Fire

"So The blades of fire are located in hell which is a bit extreme even for god" Tyler said "you don't say, hell looks exactly what i thought it would be" I replied "anyway let's get moving" so hell is a bunch of rocks that are the only thing preventing me from melting and where i have to face tons of Satan's men and since were in hell there's tons if not thousands of them spawning in an area but hey that only means more combos. After taking out the enemies a giant castle emerged "huh at least this better than the motel in my mom's home place." I entered, but as i entered hordes of enemies stabbed me all at once! Now you might think that could kill me but i just flicked one way and it broke thru the wall and after that i took out the rest of them as i already defeated tons of these guys before in the Lightning temple. I had to go through stairs and a bridge which had no walls and at the end there was a star on the floor which teleported me to the basement which is surprising that it didn't melt yet.

Never mind I wasn't in the basement I was in the 2nd half of building and there are traps up the a-- as there's these weird mouth worms wanting to bite me and spikes coming out of the ground and ceiling. At least there's a time frame you can memorize and after all of those traps and disgusting and gory scenery from the walls I made it to an arena where I found a new kind of enemy called the burners as they burn the ground when they move. My entire strategy this entire time is using the lightning claws as I decided to use them this entire time as Tyler asked me to for his research, but it's been working especially since the burners have swords which isn't that great for hand to hand combat. Besides that I smoked them with the claws. After combat i had to fly to rocks on lava and as if hell isn't pissing me off yet the last rock I landed was heading for a lava fall "oh s---"

I went but then I noticed a giant slab of rock falling then I got an idea to surf the lava so i flew towards the rock and grabbed it and began to surf the lava and only when i landed a giant wave came at me, but i just cried out "whoo-hooo" and landed and began to surf lava like a bada-- while also avoiding stone pillars and crying out some weird nonsense. Plus some tricks and i literally broke through some rocks as this is the kind of surfing where you don't want to fall into the water. After lava surfing i made it to another arena where another kind of enemy is waiting which are the flame slingers as the have bow and arrow of fire along with the previous enemies so yeah just had to take those out, the burners, and Satan's men and after your done the boss appeared which is the fire monster himself Ifrit. "You made it this far now we shall see how you fare against my flames" he said "hope better than the rest as it's hot as s--- in here" i replied "now your gonna burn more than i was originally gonna do" Ifrit said "In that case let's burn baby" and now boss battle!

This guy's pattern is that when you get close he swings his sword at you with a couple of slashes then shoots you with lava balls in this case you just gotta dodge and attack him as fast as you can which is why I'm using the claws to get in fast as you can't afford to get hit as he hits hard I mean what can you expect he's still in the lava while fighting me as if he wants to tease me by taking a bath while fighting. After he's at 50% health he fires a giant fire laser so you basically gotta dodge while he's doing this I mean it's difficult but not impossible and then he continues to do the same strategy but repeats the laser at 25% health. Eventually I defeated Ifrit and he sunk back into the lava and a giant pillar arose with the blades of fire on them. I walked toward it and grabbed them, then started slashing away with them then created a giant fire tornado that propelled me upward then slashed down in a circular motion. Then teleported out of there and about time cause I need water.

The next day at school I got the Info that Lucifer quit because he couldn't stand the kids. The girls were crying while I was beaming with absolute joy, but the principal told me that Lucifer said that this won't be the last time we'll be seeing each other which I understood to well. Tyler then told me that he actually got fired because the principal found the fact he slept WITH 300 WOMEN! "Thank god he's fired, but in all seriousness for someone known as the devil he's never going to let his eye off me" I said "Yeah that's true, but we just got to deal with 1 problem at a time and now that we dealt with that one we gotta chill" and I knew he was right so I just did that. Meanwhile in hell Satan was pissed at the failure "Does anyone know how to kill an angel kid!?" he asked his demons "maybe a bounty hunter?" 1 asked and Satan immediately killed him "That's not bad .... I need a bounty hunter and if it's one who kills angels, I know exactly who to call"

To Be Continued

GodStrike
Earth's Defender

Episode 5:Atlantis is Kraken

By Jose Nieves

PS don't worry it's free
PSS:i forgot to mention there's some mild if
not strong language

What made science class easy today was that today's topic was the lost city of Atlantis and each of our table's had a project with images and stuff you would see in your average school project, nothing special. "So i heard you're getting a project on Atlantis huh" Tyler told me later that and I responded with "yeah it's a no brainer but I'm still gonna pass it" "well with today's mission there's the possibility that you will maybe even get a higher grade" Tyler said I had no idea what exactly what he meant until he explained that the next weapon: The Trident of Water is located at the lost city of Atlantis which made a lot more sense and even more hype as that means more action and a free A+ by getting some images man Mr. Wasnock better give me that grade right now cause I'm so going to nail it especially if that trident makes me control sharks so they can eat my enemies.

"The lost city of Atlantis is located off the coast of northern Africa along with the Trident of Water" Tyler said and once I saw it, it was the most beautiful city I've ever seen especially since I can breathe under water since I'm pretty sure that God can never drown. The moment was interrupted as a bunch of sea creatures were running towards me and pass me but then I saw what were they running away from, pass the city of Atlantis was a giant motherf—ing kraken known as Hydreigon so I obviously needed to get these guys their home back and try to make sure no one breaks my camera or I'm going to lose it. So obviously there's going to be enemies waiting for me and the bad part was that that I can't use the blades of fire cause their powers don't work underwater which sucks as I just got them recently, but anyway in the water the claws of lightning deal more damage but eventually i took out more of Satan's men and continue heading towards that giant kraken with dragon heads.

The thing is that in a city there aren't a ton of platforms to jump on like Maria, so I just have to run forward and fight enemies. Speaking of enemies the next arena I faced are the levia-sharks which are a combination of a leviatien and a shark. While battling it I realized something the lightning claws actually does more damage against these creatures, so from this point on each creatures are gonna have weaknesses since the levia-shark is fully made of water you gotta use the Lightning Claws as water conducts electricity which basically means a few hit KO. After all of them were defeated a tower fall down in front of me and then even more fell down so I jumped up each of them and made it to a rooftop and each of them had like 3 enemies and each gap between the towers get longer so I had to fly over while making sure I don't hit enemies while I'm flying and then I made it into another area full of enemies like man Atlantis is seriously guarded and this time there the Aquaters.

Now the Aquaters use spears so they like to charge at you and stab you trillions of times, but to be honest I didn't really care at all as I literally just KO these water creatures in just a few hits that it's honestly a giant joke. After the enemies are all cleared the floor below me opened up and I fell down so now I have to swim down a weird tunnel which ended up me in a giant room full of water and there's a door where you need to put in a password that'll open the door. Speaking of which how does that work putting a password underwater so I have to take different tunnels that have the numbers needing to open the door, there's 4 rooms and I can't use any weapons besides my sword so yeah and if you're thinking about shocking the water it's not that simple. After battling more enemies and finding each piece of the password which is 65-37-49-10 and after putting that in the door opened and the water pushed me and I was enjoying it by sliding into the surface and after getting up in front of me was Hydreigon the dragon headed Kraken.

"You must be the wrenched fiend Godstrike" Hydegion said and I replied with "you know that's funny I get that a lot, and where you heard about me, your girlfriends you never had" "INSULT ME ONE MORE TIME AND I'll MAKE YOU SUFFER MORE THAN YOU THOUGHT IMAGINABLE" he said furiously "In that case let's try, c'mon" I replied Boss battle time. The strategy with this is that he shoots balls out of his infinite amount of tentacle dragon heads then he breaks the floor with its head then tries to bite me like am I that delicious. When he's at 50% percent health he fires balls of ink from the octopus part which would blind me for like a minute but after that along with the original strategy the dragon head tentacles charge at me from all corner left,right,front and behind but i forgot to mention when the dragon heads pop out and miss the bite then slash away and you can also shoot projectiles when the dragon tentacles charge and it he repeats the ink balls at 25% as well.

After the giant Abomination was defeated he exploded like the rest and the Water trident came out, I grabbed it and began jabbing away and thank god IT CONTROLS SHARKS! Before I teleported out of there I took some pictures for my project and afterwards I teleported back home to work on my project where I eventually got an A. Meanwhile in Satan's bar, the assassin came into the room "Gladius, how's your recent job" Satan asked "alright" he replied "Btw could you pass me the bottle of Vodka" Satan demanded and Gladius fired a shot that killed multiple demons and passed the vodka "Well then it's time to pay the assassin! Seriously, get my god d--- checkbook!" Satan demanded as he called to his demons while Gladius set his guns to angel kill Mode.

To Be Continued

Godstrike

Episode 6: Sharpshooter Gladius

Warning:Cursing

PS:this has nothing to do with any other
product, Just the title

Author: Jose Nieves

It was a peaceful afternoon as Tyler and I were gazing into the sky looking at the clouds "You know this feels nice to just relax and do absolutely Nothing" I sighed "You said it I don't what could possibly could go wrong in this peaceful afternoon" but speak of the devil as we were awaken by the sound of a violent whistle "WAKE UP! How dare you fall asleep in my class" the gym teacher yelled violently and made us do multiple exercises like jumping jacks, Pushups and I fell after doing 1 and wall sits in front of the entire gym class, some laughed, others mocked and others joined because bros go through hardship together considering that were all basically single and we have to stay together, but then there was a bigger problem.

You see the final part of our punishment exercises involved running around the track multiple times while the gym teacher said stuff like "Come on bruskies show us your men!" "please god send a distraction" I whispered but suddenly I heard the noise of a helicopter coming closer and closer and I saw some dude jump out, but as things couldn't get any more bizarre he pulls out a massive gun and makes it rain energy blast destroying the windows "oh WHY!" I yelled as people evacuated and the dude landed on the ground and it was the assassin Gladius "Never thought I would have to kill a kid" He sighed "what are you talking about?" I asked "My employer who you might know known as Lucifer hired me, the name's Gladius and I've been assigned to assassinate you".

This dude fires Aura blast out of his guns in many directions and I'm Just dodging while he's trying to land a hit but suddenly his guns changed and now he can fire more which made it harder to dodge. As if that wasn't crazy enough his guns now turn into canons and they hit hard as I flew back 10 feet. "The fact that you survived a blast like that confirms my suspicions, you are Godstrike." Before he could blast my a-- off he heard a siren and it was the cops so he had to leave, but I was pissed afterwards. That night I was ranting on my embarrassing loss to Tyler "I can't believe I got my butt kicked by an assassin" I said "Bounty Hunter" Tyler interrupted "Whatever what I really need is some serious firepower" I demanded "Which is why I made these" Tyler announced as he unveiled his greatest Invention "Behold .454 casual fully automatics, and the best part they use infinite Bullets just use your Aura and fire" he explained "Tyler you are a lot of things, but above all you're a genius" I complimented.

Now Aura is the power system of this world as its the spiritual energy of the human being that can be used in many ways: Creation, Element, Heal, Projectile And Strength. I already learned Element, Heal, and strength from god before fighting Darkron, so now I had to master Projectile on weapons and it took a while like 10 hours to master it before meeting Gladius. I was waiting at Baltimore before he appeared "This time the police won't be helping you out kid" He said "trust me I'm ready" I responded and we rushed towards each other running across rooftop to rooftop shooting at each other while destroying many different areas until eventually redirected all of his shots to him and finished him off. He was on the ground now you think that I would kill him but he's human not a demon so I asked "Can we discuss business"

Now we went to a 5 star bar and I paid for his drink. We discussed a good agreement as I handed him a suitcase double the amount of money he was paid for and decided to leave me alone. At school Tyler asked "Did you handle him?" "Yeah but I didn't kill him, I paid him after all the best weapon to use is your brain" I confirmed "well is nice to know you're being mature" Tyler sighed. Meanwhile in Satan's bar he begins to think "well that went absolutely poorly, but that doesn't matter as there's a much bigger threat coming and I'm all for it" he says as he looks into space as a group of ships are coming to wreak havoc.

To Be continued

Thank you so
much for the support

LoveLN

Made in the USA
Middletown, DE
22 March 2022

63016315R00027